Printed in the United States of America

Sunny Day Publishing, LLC
Cuyahoga Falls, Ohio 44223
www.sunnydaypublishing.com

ISBN 978-0-9978006-8-5
Library of Congress Control Number: 2016960078

SUNNY DAY®
PUBLISHING, LLC

This book is dedicated to my son Caleb.
Thank you for making my dreams come true.
I love you!

-Mom

There once was a tiny little mouse
who found a gingerbread house.
His name was Charlie.

He wanted to explore,
so he opened the door

and to his surprise,
found goodies inside.

Charlie saw sprinkles
that looked like snow

and ate gooey gumdrops
that stuck to his nose.

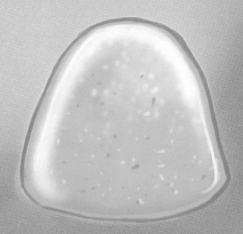

He licked peppermint sticks
and lemon drops

and then he hopped off
to eat lollipops.

Jelly beans! Gummy bears!
Marshmallow fluff was
everywhere!

The house was filled
with so many yummies,
he couldn't help but
fill up his tummy.

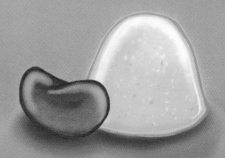

So he ate the ceiling
and he ate the floor
till Charlie's Gingerbread House
was no more.

82562813R10015

Made in the USA
Columbia, SC
04 December 2017